JoJo & Bow Bow
TAKE THE STAGE

BY JoJo Siwa

nickelodeon.

AMULET BOOKS
NEW YORK

Cataloging-in-Publication Data has been applied for and may be obtained from the Library of Congress.

ISBN 978-1-4197-3601-8

Amulet Books are available at special discounts when purchased in quantity for premiums and promotions as well as fundraising or educational use. Special editions can also be created to specification. For details, contact specialsales@abramsbooks.com or the address below.

ABRAMS The Art of Books
195 Broadway, New York, NY 10007
abramsbooks.com

CONTENTS

✱ ⬦ ✱

✱ ⬦ ✱

CHAPTER 1

JoJo Siwa had just heard the best news. It was so amazing, she couldn't decide who to share it with first—her adorable teacup Yorkie, BowBow, or her very best friend in the whole world, Miley. She glanced toward her nightstand, where her phone was charging. It would take just a few seconds to dash off a text to Miley. *Decision made.* As she reached for her glitter phone case, JoJo heard a familiar sound.

Thump, thump, thump. JoJo looked down from where she was sitting cross-legged on her pink bedspread and saw BowBow wagging her tail and looking up at her expectantly from the floor. Being the adorable little teacup she was, BowBow was too small to jump up onto the bed. But by thumping her tail against it, she was letting JoJo know she needed a lift.

JoJo scooped BowBow into her arms, then settled back against her mountain of fuzzy pink pillows, BowBow in her lap.

"Okay, BowBow, I have to text Miley really quick, and then I have some super exciting news to share with you!"

JoJo typed her message to her best friend, adding a few heart emojis, and pressed Send. Putting her phone down, she turned her attention back to BowBow.

"Are you ready for the super exciting news?" JoJo asked.

BowBow licked JoJo's chin. She was ready.

"So, I just found out that there's going to be a block party on our street in two weeks! Do you know what a block party is, Bow-Bow?" BowBow wagged her tail and tilted her head to the right, which JoJo was pretty sure meant, "No, but please continue."

"A block party is a huge party thrown by the entire neighborhood. Everyone is invited, and everyone comes together to hang out and have fun. There will be a bouncy house and cotton candy machine and snow cones and pizza and games. Definitely my kind of party!" JoJo was speaking really fast, something she did when she was excited. And she got excited a *lot*, so BowBow was really good at following along. "There'll even

3

be an outdoor movie with a big projector and face painting and other kinds of entertainment. Speaking of entertainment, I just had an *amazing* idea . . ."

BowBow perked up. She was definitely excited about JoJo's idea! She jumped off JoJo's lap and began running back and forth on the bed to show exactly how excited she was.

JoJo leapt up too, scooting off her bed to pace back and forth in her room, her brilliant plan churning around and around in her head. She had to talk about it with Miley before she burst!

Just then, her phone rang. JoJo's face broke into a wide grin. She didn't even have to look at the screen to know who was calling—the personalized "Kid in a Candy Store" ringtone had tipped her off. It was Miley, of course!

"Miley, did you get my text?" JoJo asked breathlessly.

At the same exact time, Miley said, "JoJo, I just got your text!"

"Jinx! Kind of," said JoJo. The two best friends cracked up, and Miley even let out her signature snort-giggle.

"You first!" Miley said.

"No! You called me, so you can go first," JoJo replied.

"Yeah, but you had the big news, so . . ."

"Okay, I can't take it anymore!" JoJo said excitedly. "So, you got my text about the block party. Cool, right? Everyone is invited! And if that's not the *best* kind of party, I don't know what is, amiright?" JoJo was talking fast again, but Miley was just as good as Bow-Bow at following along when JoJo got started. They'd been best friends for so long, they practically had their own language. "Anyway, I was talking to BowBow about how there's going to be entertainment there—"

"Wait, what?" Miley interrupted, her voice playful. "You were discussing the block party with BowBow? Your *dog*, BowBow?"

JoJo couldn't believe her ears. Was Miley suggesting that . . . BowBow *didn't understand*?

"Um, of course I was discussing it with BowBow! Are you trying to suggest that my cute little dog doesn't speak Human?" JoJo asked in her most dramatic voice.

"Of course I wasn't saying that!" Miley's grin shone through her words. "I was just surprised that you were discussing it with BowBow before me!"

JoJo giggled. She knew Miley was kidding. Even so, she never missed a chance to tell her friends how special they were to her. "You know I love you, Miley!" she said sincerely.

"And if you promise not to brag about it . . . I did text you first, before I even told BowBow about the block party."

"Awww. Thanks, girl." Miley laughed. "So wait, go on. What about the entertainment?"

"Right." JoJo felt herself getting worked up again. "I had the best idea. Are you ready?" She didn't even pause to hear Miley's response. "What if I perform at the block party? And I was thinking maybe you could help me choreograph a new dance number for my performance! We have two weeks to come up with something, which isn't a ton of time, but I know we can do it. What do you say?"

"What do I say?" Miley asked, pretending she needed to consider it. "Hmm, I don't know . . ." JoJo could imagine Miley on the other end of the phone, deep in thought, twirling a strand of her long, curly hair around her finger.

This time, JoJo really thought she might burst. She knew Miley loved to tease, but she still bounced up and down on her toes while waiting for Miley's official yes. Her best friend was really great at choreography, and JoJo couldn't think of a better way to involve Miley in her performance than having her help design her routine!

After what felt like an eternity . . .

"That sounds like the Best. Idea. Ever!" Miley finally exclaimed. "I would *love* to help choreograph your performance! And, JoJo, so many kids from school are *huge* fans of yours—half of them have 'Boomerang' as their ringtone! I know they would love to see you perform!"

Since JoJo had been homeschooled for practically her whole life, she didn't know all the neighborhood kids, but planning a performance at the block party seemed like a perfect way to meet them *and* make some new friends. There were few things JoJo loved more than making new friends!

"Yay!" JoJo cheered. "This is going to be so fun! Let's get together tomorrow to start figuring it all out! Oh, and let's invite Jacob too!"

"Definitely," Miley agreed.

Jacob went to school with Miley and was close friends with both girls. JoJo's mom, Jessalynn, sometimes referred to them as "The Three Musketeers" because they loved hanging out together so much. JoJo and Miley and Jacob had never seen or read *The Three Musketeers*, but they knew it meant they were BFFs.

After getting off the phone with Miley, JoJo started to fill BowBow in on her plans. But then she realized BowBow had been listening the whole time. She just had one question for her frisky little pup:

"BowBow, are you ready to take the stage?"

CHAPTER 2

"Which bow do you feel like wearing today, BowBow?" JoJo asked.

It was the following afternoon, and JoJo and BowBow were getting ready to head over to Miley's.

"Yellow polka dots?" JoJo held up a small yellow bow in one hand. "Or pink tie-dye to match me?"

BowBow yipped excitedly as JoJo dangled

the pink bow that was a miniature version of the one she was wearing.

"Good choice!" JoJo said. She gently attached the bow to a tuft of fur at the top of BowBow's adorable little head. Some days they matched their bows exactly, and other days they didn't. JoJo usually let BowBow decide, but occasionally she had to overrule her if BowBow chose a bow that really didn't go well with JoJo's. Luckily that didn't happen very often. JoJo's bows were made to be the best, brightest, cutest accessories. They usually went with anything at all!

After saying goodbye to her mom and promising to be home in time for dinner, JoJo and BowBow set out for Miley's house, which was just a few blocks away. JoJo sometimes rode her bike there, but today she felt like walking. From the way BowBow happily wagged her tail when JoJo clipped her hot-pink leash to her collar, it seemed that Bow-Bow agreed that a walk was a good idea.

As they turned at the end of their block, JoJo felt a gentle tugging on the leash as Bow-Bow tried to pull her across the street.

"That isn't Miley's house." JoJo laughed as BowBow pressed on toward a Spanish-style house. As they got closer, JoJo noticed a girl who looked to be about her age walking up the driveway.

"Hi there," JoJo called, waving. "My dog, BowBow"—she dissolved into giggles as BowBow tugged her way toward the girl—"is apparently very excited to meet you!"

The girl crouched down in the driveway and let BowBow sniff her hand. Then she gently pet the little Yorkie on the head.

"I'm JoJo," JoJo said, smiling at the red-haired girl BowBow seemed to like so much.

"I—I know who you are," the girl stammered. As she looked up, JoJo could see she was blushing.

"Are you new to the neighborhood? I don't think I've seen you before."

"I am. We just moved in last week," the girl replied, tucking a strand of wavy red hair behind her ear. "I'm Grace."

JoJo could tell that Grace was shy. Sometimes when she met new kids, they were especially shy around her because they were fans of her songs and YouTube channel, and they got a little starstruck. When that happened, JoJo tried extra hard to put them at ease.

"I love your unicorn shirt," JoJo said, gesturing to the pale yellow T-shirt Grace was wearing with denim shorts and glittery flip-flops. Just then, BowBow yipped as if she were agreeing with JoJo about Grace's shirt.

Both girls laughed. "I think BowBow likes it too," JoJo added between giggles. Unicorns were everything.

Grace grinned happily, revealing bright pink braces. "Thanks—I love unicorns. They're kind of my thing."

"Very cool." JoJo nodded. "Like bows are kind of my thing!" She gestured to the tie-dyed bow with rhinestones attached to her ponytail.

With the ice broken, JoJo and Grace fell into an easy conversation. Grace asked about the local school, and when JoJo explained that she was homeschooled, Grace looked disappointed. "I was hoping you went to my school . . . ," Grace explained after a moment. "It would have been nice to know some-one on my first day. But it's cool that you're homeschooled!"

"Yeah, it is pretty great," JoJo agreed.

"But as for knowing someone at school, you have nothing to worry about. My two closest friends, Miley and Jacob, go there! You can meet them, and then you'll know *two* people! In fact, I was just on my way over to Miley's house now. Why don't you come with?"

"Really?" Grace asked. "I— That's so nice of you to offer. Are you sure?"

"Of course I'm sure!" JoJo exclaimed.

While Grace went inside to ask her mom if it was okay to go to Miley's, JoJo texted Miley to let her know she was bringing a new friend with her. Miley sent her the thumbs-up emoji, and Grace returned a few moments later, smiling from ear to ear. Her mom, from whom Grace seemed to have inherited her pretty red hair, waved from the front door. "Text me to let me know you arrived safely," she called.

"Will do, Mom!" Grace replied.

On their way to Miley's, JoJo filled Grace in on the upcoming block party. She was just getting to the part about her performance when they reached Miley's front door. As JoJo raised her hand to knock, the door flew open. BowBow jumped excitedly as she spotted Miley, who was probably her second favorite person after JoJo.

"I was waiting at the window because I'm so excited to talk about the block party!" Miley exclaimed, her voice muffled slightly as she hugged her best friend. "And you must be Grace," she said a moment later as she separated from JoJo. "So nice to meet you! Welcome to the neighborhood!"

Before Grace could answer, Miley enveloped her in a hug.

With her caramel-colored skin still showing hints of the tan she'd picked up on the beach vacation she'd taken with her family a few weeks ago, and with her long, curly hair rocking natural highlights from the sun, JoJo's best friend was looking even cuter than usual. Miley was as pretty on the outside as she was on the inside.

"She's a bit of a hugger," JoJo pretended to whisper to Grace. "It's kind of her thing!"

BowBow yipped as if to say, "What about me?" and all three girls burst into laughter. "Oh, hello to you too, BowBow," Miley cooed as she bent over to scoop up BowBow and give her a hug.

"Ahem." Jacob appeared behind Miley, pretending to clear his throat.

"And this is Jacob," JoJo said as Jacob stepped into view and gave Grace a little wave. Jacob was a full head taller than Miley. He'd had a big growth spurt over the summer. "He's just as awesome as Miley but way less huggy."

Grace smiled and waved back.

"Cool braces," Jacob said, running a hand through his shaggy dark hair. Jacob had always worn his hair really short, but for the past few months he'd been growing it out. He'd told JoJo and Miley that he had a certain look in mind, but they still weren't quite sure what that look was, so they loved to joke with him about it. That was the kind of friendship the girls had with Jacob, and it was no secret that he loved their good-natured teasing.

Jacob turned to JoJo. "Bonus points for making a new friend with *braces*," he said, wiggling his eyebrows as he emphasized the last word.

"Oh, no," Miley said as JoJo sighed.

Grace looked from Jacob to Miley and finally to JoJo, a confused look on her face.

"Grace, I apologize now for the fact that Jacob is probably going to grill you all day about your braces," JoJo explained. "He's getting braces soon, and he's sort of obsessed with talking about them."

"Knowledge is power," Jacob said, shrugging.

Grace burst out laughing. "No problem at all—I was really curious too before I got them. Ask away!"

"I like her already!" Jacob grinned. "Miley, invite this girl inside!"

"Right, don't mind me!" Miley giggled. "Please come in! There's plenty of snacks in the kitchen." She gestured for the girls to come inside and then placed BowBow back down on the ground. "Jacob brought over homemade brownies!" she added, clapping excitedly.

"Homemade brownies by Jacob? Lead the way!" JoJo cheered as she unclipped Bow-Bow's leash. She smiled encouragingly at

Grace. Meeting three new people all in one day could be a lot for a shy person, but JoJo was determined to make sure Grace felt right at home with her and her friends.

A little while later, JoJo knew she had nothing to worry about, because Grace fit in perfectly with their little group. She was a great sport about Jacob grilling her about her braces, and, JoJo realized, all Jacob's silly questions had really helped put Grace at ease.

Just then, Miley's mom poked her head into the kitchen. "I know Jacob brought over brownies, but we also have cake pops if anyone is interested . . ."

"Is that even a question?" Jacob asked as the three girls nodded.

A few moments later, Mrs. Bryant placed a plate of four cake pops in the center of the table, along with a stack of napkins. The kids all thanked her and then immediately reached out to claim a cake pop.

"So you can eat cake pops with braces?" Jacob asked excitedly as Grace took a delicate bite of hers.

"Jacob, why *wouldn't* you be able to eat cake pops with braces?" Miley asked.

"I don't know." Jacob grinned as the girls all laughed. "I'm just glad to know you can."

"Okay, maybe we should get down to work and talk about the block party and figure out what we're all doing," JoJo said a moment later. JoJo loved goofing around with her friends, but she also knew when it was time to buckle down. "Order in the kitchen!" She pretended to pound her cake pop like a gavel on her napkin. "I know I'm going to perform, and Miley is going to help me choreograph. What do you guys think you want to do?"

"I'm thinking I can help out with the food

in some way," Jacob replied. "Making it or selling it or both. Whatever they need."

"Jacob loves food," JoJo explained to Grace. "As you can tell from the brownies, he's an incredible baker."

"They were *really* good!" Grace agreed.

"What about you?" Miley asked Grace. "What are you amazing at?

Grace's cheeks turned red. "I—I don't think I'm really great at anything," she said finally.

"I do not believe that for one second!" JoJo declared. "Everyone is really good at something! What do you *like* to do?"

"Well . . ." Grace looked at the friendly faces around the table. JoJo smiled encouragingly. "I—I like art. Painting and drawing and stuff. And I guess I'm okay at it . . ."

"That's so cool!" JoJo exclaimed.

"Definitely!" Miley nodded.

"Now I know who to ask for help with my art projects next year," Jacob added.

Grace flushed with happiness. "For sure," she told Jacob.

"You can pay her in brownies!" JoJo quipped, and everyone laughed. "But joking aside, that is an amazing talent to have! We just need to figure out how to put it to good use at the block party . . ."

"Speaking of which," Miley said, waving her own cake pop for emphasis. "This girl from school, Kyra, just texted me to say that her mom is the head of the block party committee, so she invited us over tomorrow to talk about what we kids can do."

"Great!" JoJo exclaimed. "I don't think I've heard you mention Kyra before, have I?"

"She just started at our school at the end of last year," Jacob explained.

Miley, whose mouth was full of cake pop,

nodded. "She wasn't in our homeroom, so we don't know her very well yet."

"So after tomorrow, you'll know *three* people at your new school!" JoJo said to Grace. "And maybe Kyra will have a great idea of how to put your art skills to good use at the block party."

"Oh, do you think it's okay if I come too?" Grace asked.

"Sure, it's okay!" Miley smiled. "Kyra said to invite my friends. And you're my friend, so that means you're invited!"

JoJo took a sip of her lemonade and looked around the kitchen table at her friends. Miley and Jacob were the two best friends a girl could ever ask for. JoJo loved that they embraced making new friends as much as she did. And she was really glad she'd bumped into Grace. She had a feeling this was the beginning of a wonderful new friendship.

CHAPTER 3

The next day, JoJo, Miley, Jacob, and Grace met up in front of Miley's house.

"Kyra's house is that green one on the corner," Miley said, pointing to a home down the block that was set back from the street, a winding driveway leading up to it.

"I think you might have some competition for BowBow's second favorite person," JoJo teased Miley as they walked. BowBow had been so excited to see Grace that she had jumped up and down until Grace scooped her up to give her a kiss hello. She was now carrying the little Yorkie the rest of the way to Kyra's house.

"Oh, I'm sure she was just excited to see me because I'm new to the group," Grace said quickly. She looked at Miley to see if Miley was upset, but Miley was grinning.

"Luckily, I don't mind sharing," Miley told Grace. "And if you do officially replace me in BowBow's heart, you can make it up to me by lending me that adorable unicorn necklace you're wearing. I love it!"

"Deal!" Grace agreed happily. The necklace was a silver, sparkly unicorn with a rainbow horn. It was her favorite, but she was always happy to share with a friend. Having a friend to share with in her new town made her shiver with happiness.

"You guys do realize that I'm actually

BowBow's second favorite person, right?" Jacob broke in. "I've asked her not to be obvious about it, but she thinks I'm the best human after JoJo."

"If that's true, it's probably because she associates you with food!" JoJo replied without missing a beat.

Jacob clutched his chest as if he had been wounded, and JoJo, Grace, and Miley cracked up.

Miley rang Kyra's doorbell, and a moment later the door swung open. A girl with long, dark hair stood there, a smile lighting her features. Her brown eyes swept the group, and JoJo thought she saw her frown slightly when they landed on Grace and BowBow.

I hope it's okay that I brought BowBow along, JoJo thought. *I forgot to ask if she was allergic!*

But as Miley made quick introductions,

the frown JoJo had noticed disappeared, and Kyra smiled warmly and invited everyone inside, explaining that they would be meeting on the back porch.

"I'm a really big fan of yours," Kyra said, falling into step beside JoJo as the group walked through the house. "It's so exciting to meet you! I saw the Nickelodeon Kids' Choice Awards the last two years and loved your outfits!"

"Aw, thank you! It's really nice to meet you too!" JoJo replied. "I realized I probably should have asked in advance if it was okay to bring my dog," she added. "I can run her home if it's a problem . . ."

"Oh, it's no problem at all," Kyra assured her as they stepped onto the enclosed porch. "I love dogs! So, she's yours and not Grace's?"

"Yep, BowBow is mine," JoJo replied. "She

just really loves Grace, so Grace carried her here," she explained as she settled into a chair.

Kyra sat down in the chair next to JoJo's. Jacob, Miley, and Grace were already seated. JoJo could tell that Kyra was nervous, and JoJo wanted to do everything she could to put her at ease. She knew it could be hard encountering four relatively new kids all at once.

"Are those cookies I see?" JoJo asked, pointing to a plate full of yellow-frosted stars and hearts on the table.

Kyra nodded eagerly. "Yes, we have cookies. My mom made them. And we have other stuff inside too, if you don't like cookies. Ice cream? Chips?"

"Who doesn't love cookies?" Jacob asked, helping himself to two.

Kyra looked at JoJo and Miley. "Are cookies

okay with you too? I can get you something else . . ."

"Cookies are perfect," JoJo replied. "I just ate lunch, though. But I knew Jacob would be all over them."

"So, Grace," Kyra said a moment later. "I don't think I recognize you from school."

"Oh, I just moved here," Grace explained.

"How do you know everyone already?" Kyra asked.

"Well . . . my good luck, I guess," Grace replied. "I bumped into JoJo yesterday when she was on her way to Miley's house, and she invited me to tag along. I just met everyone yesterday."

"Oh, so you're new too?" Kyra asked, her voice a little flat.

"Yeah, I'm even newer than you," Grace said. She smiled warmly at Kyra, but Kyra's face clouded over.

"I forgot the drinks," she said a moment later, frowning. "Is seltzer okay with everyone?"

Before anyone could answer, Kyra rose up out of her chair and headed into the kitchen.

"I'll go help her carry everything," Miley said a moment later, after exchanging a look with JoJo.

The girls returned a few minutes later, Kyra's mom right behind them.

"Hi, kids," Mrs. Gregory said, smiling warmly at the group. "I just wanted to welcome you all here and say thank you for helping out with the block party. Kyra and I really appreciate it!"

"We're happy to help," JoJo said, returning the smile.

"Yeah," Miley echoed. "And thank you for the cookies!"

Grace and Jacob murmured thanks as

well, and Mrs. Gregory waved a hand. "It was nothing. Please enjoy! Kyra, I'll be in my office if you need me. Have fun," she called over her shoulder as she walked back into the house.

"I might have to get this cookie recipe from your mom," Jacob told Kyra as he stuffed the rest of his first cookie into his mouth.

"For sure!"

As everyone around the table cracked open their cans of sparkling water, JoJo asked Kyra about the block party. She was still trying to put Kyra at ease, and she thought that getting her to talk about the block party—the reason she had invited them all over—might help her loosen up a little bit.

Kyra explained that the block party was going to span three whole blocks in their neighborhood, and they were expecting people from all over town to attend. Her mom was the head of the planning committee and had asked her to be in charge of the entertainment, except for the evening movie, which was already being taken care of by some volunteers from the high school. "And that's where you guys come in," Kyra said. "JoJo, I was kind of hoping you might want to perform . . . ? I know it's a lot to ask, but you have so many local fans, and a performance from you would be the highlight of the whole day!"

"Well, great minds think alike! Because I was going to tell you that I would *love* to perform!" JoJo replied. "And Miley is going to help me choreograph a new dance number for the performance."

"That sounds amazing!" Kyra cheered. "And, Miley, that's so cool that you're a choreographer!"

"And she's *so* good at it!" JoJo said, smiling proudly at her best friend.

"Okay, let's see, what else . . . ?" Kyra mumbled as she jotted notes on a piece of paper. "Jacob, what would you like to do? Any interest in handling the balloon animals?"

Jacob grimaced slightly. "I get kind of freaked out by the sound of popping balloons," he admitted sheepishly. "Can I do something else?"

"Of course!" Kyra said quickly. "What would you like to do?"

"Well, I love food—cooking it and eating it . . ." As if to prove his point, Jacob took a huge bite of his remaining cookie. "So I was going to offer to help out with refreshments. But I don't have to—I can do something in the entertainment category."

"No worries—I'll put you down for refreshments!" Kyra waved a hand. "I'll let my mom know—I'm sure they'll be grateful for the help." Kyra reached for a cookie, took a small bite, and then continued speaking. "I'll take care of everything else related to your performance, JoJo," she decided.

"That's a *really* big job," JoJo replied. "I mean, so much goes into planning something like that. Hiring a sound truck, getting all the equipment ready, creating a flyer advertising the performance . . . it's a lot for one person. I was going to suggest that my mom call your mom and they could figure it out together. My mom has a lot of experience dealing with all that."

"That's great." Kyra nodded. "But I'll still be the main organizer for it."

"Are you sure?" JoJo asked. "It's really a lot for one person to do. And you have so much to be responsible for, being in charge of all the entertainment . . ."

"I'd be happy to help out!" Grace volunteered. "I don't have anything to do yet, and I'm really organized, so maybe I can help you."

"I'm *super* organized and won't need help," Kyra replied, her tone a little harsh. Then her voice softened, and she smiled. "I'm sorry—I appreciate the offer, Grace," she said firmly. "I just know I can handle it myself. Don't worry, JoJo," she added. "I won't let you down!"

Miley jumped into the conversation and told Kyra that she was thinking of teaching a dance class at the block party. "Wouldn't it be cool to teach kids the dance steps JoJo will be performing so they can dance along from the audience?"

"I love that idea!" Kyra said excitedly. "Your dance class will be the hit of the block party—next to JoJo's performance, of course!"

Next to JoJo, Grace cleared her throat quietly. "So . . . what can I do to help?" she asked.

Kyra looked at the piece of paper in front

of her and frowned. "There's really not much else. I think you can just show up and enjoy yourself!"

"What about the balloon animals?" Grace asked, a crestfallen look on her face. "Don't you need someone to do those? I could learn how and help out with that."

"Oh, don't worry," Kyra said, shrugging. "I just remembered that my mom said some kids from the high school were willing to help out, and I bet I can get them to do the balloon animals."

"Oh, okay," Grace replied.

"Um, Grace is really good at art," JoJo said, nudging her friend gently, hoping she would speak up. JoJo could tell Grace wanted to do *something* at the block party; she hoped she would tell Kyra that. But Grace remained silent.

"Yeah, Grace is a great artist, and we were

trying to think of something she could do at the block party to put her talent to good use," Jacob added.

"Hmm, that's a tough one...," Kyra replied, tapping her pencil on the table. "I mean, we'll have face painting, but I was going to do that. I've already started researching how to do it online."

"I've got it!" Miley said suddenly, snapping her fingers. "What about if Grace draws portraits? Fairs always have those portrait stands...we should have one at our block party too! What do you think, Grace?"

Grace beamed excitedly. "Drawing portraits is actually one of my favorite things to do!" she exclaimed. "And I'm pretty good at it too," she added shyly.

"Great idea, Miley!" JoJo cheered.

"Yeah, great idea," Kyra repeated. But she sounded just a little less excited than JoJo.

CHAPTER 4

It sounds like the block party is going to be soooo much fun!" JoJo said to her friends as the group walked home from Kyra's. "I think I'm most excited about the bouncy house! I'm going to be all over that!"

"Me too!" Jacob said. Then, catching the looks Miley and JoJo were giving him, he held up his hands. "I promise not to go in after stuffing my face on pizza," he added solemnly. "Don't ask," he told Grace, who had raised her eyebrows in his direction.

As Miley and JoJo burst out laughing, Grace made a face. "I think I can use my imagination to figure out what happened," she joked.

"I love your idea of using the dance class to teach my routine to everyone," JoJo said to Miley a moment later. "It will be so great to have people in the audience dancing along with me!"

"Yeah, about that," Jacob said, looking at Miley. "Do you really think people are going to be able to pick up a complicated dance routine like the kind JoJo performs?"

"I was a little worried about that too," Grace added. "I'm not the greatest dancer, and I don't think I can dance the way JoJo does."

"Oh, don't worry," Miley assured her friends. "I'll come up with a less complicated routine for the class so everyone can join in!

I should have explained that—I definitely don't expect everyone to be able to do what JoJo does!"

"As long as people are willing to get up, move around, and have fun, it will be great!" JoJo added. "That's what dancing is all about, right?"

A few steps later, they had arrived at Miley's house. "I have to head in," Miley said apologetically. "I'd invite you guys in, but I promised my mom I'd come straight home after Kyra's. I think we're going to my aunt's house or something." She gave each of her friends a goodbye hug.

"Aw, no worries," JoJo said, returning Miley's hug. "I was just going to ask if anyone wants to come hang out at my house for a bit . . . ?"

"No can do," Jacob replied. "I have to head home to go to the orthodontist. I'm getting spacers put in today!"

JoJo nodded. "How about you, Grace? Can you come hang out for a bit?"

"I think so!" A shy, happy smile lit up Grace's face. "Let me call my mom and ask."

"Text me later," Miley said to JoJo as she headed inside.

"You know it!" JoJo called after her. "Say hi to your aunt for me!"

By the time Jacob said his goodbyes and headed off in the opposite direction toward his house, Grace was off the phone with her mom. "She said it's fine for me to go over for a bit."

JoJo grinned. "Great, let's go!"

A little while later, Grace and JoJo were seated by the pool in JoJo's backyard, dangling their legs in the water.

"Thanks so much for including me today," Grace said shyly as she swirled her feet around in the water. "I'm so glad I met you! Before yesterday, I was pretty nervous about starting at a new school. I kind of had a hard time making friends at my old school," she confided. "And I was worried it was going to be the same thing here."

"Well, you have nothing to worry about," JoJo assured her. "You already have three—no, make that four—friends in your new town!"

Grace smiled and let out a nervous breath. "I was wondering . . . ," she said slowly. "Do you think Kyra likes me?"

JoJo pulled one foot out of the pool and turned so she could face her friend. "Sure. Why wouldn't she?"

"I don't know." Grace shrugged and looked at the water. "It might have been my imagination, but I felt like maybe I did something wrong to make her not like me."

"Of course you didn't do anything wrong,"

JoJo said gently. "I think Kyra was just a little overwhelmed by meeting so many new people. Don't forget, she barely knew Jacob and Miley before today either."

"I can definitely understand that," Grace replied. She smiled again, this time more confidently. "I'm sure you're right. I keep forgetting that Kyra is new to this town too. She was probably feeling a little nervous about meeting everyone."

"Exactly," JoJo agreed, careful to keep her voice upbeat.

A little while later, after Grace had left, JoJo sat cross-legged on the floor of her room, playing fetch with BowBow. She tossed the palm-sized, orange bouncy ball against the wall, and it ricocheted into her closet, disappearing amid a pile of bedazzled sneakers. JoJo laughed as BowBow leapt right into the sneaker stack to retrieve it, her little butt in the air, tail wagging.

Playtime with her pup was always JoJo's favorite, but this time she couldn't shake her worry. Grace's words had been on her mind ever since their conversation, and JoJo couldn't help but admit Grace had a point. As much as JoJo wanted to believe the best in everyone, Kyra had seemed a little . . . *off* that day. JoJo sighed; she just wanted everyone to be friends, but she couldn't help wondering if Grace had been right. As if she knew JoJo was worried, BowBow bounded over and dropped the ball in front of her.

"You found it! Good girl," JoJo exclaimed. BowBow leapt into JoJo's lap, licking her cheek as JoJo cuddled her close. "Ew!" said JoJo, when BowBow went for her mouth. "No more kisses!" BowBow let out a bark and jumped from her lap, bounding for the door, where she paused and looked back at JoJo, her head tilted to one side. That was a sign that she wanted to go outside and play some more. "Okay, okay," JoJo said, pulling herself to her feet. "You're right! It's a beautiful day—let's get some fresh air and clear our heads."

No matter what the situation, BowBow always knew how to put things in perspective.

That evening, over dinner, JoJo filled her family in on what she had learned about the block party.

"It's going to be so cool!" she explained breathlessly. "There will be snow cones *and* an ice cream truck, plus a million other food options, face painting by Kyra, portraits by Grace, a dance lesson by Miley, and . . ." JoJo paused to take a breath. "A bouncy house, tons of games, balloon animals . . . what am I forgetting?"

"A performance by JoJo Siwa?" JoJo's brother, Jayden, said after a moment. "Don't forget that!"

"Oh, yeah, of course!" JoJo laughed. "Which reminds me . . . Mom, Kyra wants to be in charge of planning *everything* for my performance, but I said I thought you could call her mom and talk everything through . . ."

"Already on it," her mom replied. "I spoke to Kyra's mom this afternoon, and we talked about everything that needs to be done. Aside from the flyers, which I think she's depending on Kyra to create, it's all under control."

"Great." JoJo breathed a sigh of relief. She believed Kyra when she said she was super organized, but JoJo had been performing for a while—big shows, small shows, and everything in between. She knew by now that it involved way too much work for one person to do by herself! JoJo was glad her mom was going to help.

As JoJo's dad and Jayden began clearing the dishes from the dinner table, JoJo went into the kitchen with her mom to help load the dishwasher. They had a routine: Her mom would rinse and hand the dishes to JoJo, who would load them into the dishwasher. And BowBow supervised, cleaning up any stray crumbs.

"So it sounds like you've made two new friends this week," Mrs. Siwa said as she handed a glass to JoJo. "The Three Musketeers are expanding!"

JoJo filled her mom in on how she had bumped into Grace the day before while on her way over to Miley's house. "She's super sweet," she said. "A little shy, but once she opens up, she's really fun and funny. I'm so glad I met her!"

"And how about Kyra?" Mrs. Siwa asked. "Her mom mentioned they are relatively new to town. Was this her first time meeting Miley and Jacob as well?"

JoJo explained how Kyra had moved to the town a few months ago but still didn't know many people. "Our get-together was actually a little awkward today. Kyra was pretty tense, like she was trying *really* hard." JoJo frowned as she tried to think of the right way to describe how Kyra had acted. She handed a salad plate back to her mom because it still had a blob of lettuce stuck to it. "This needs another rinse. But Kyra seems really cool too. I think she was just nervous and wanted everyone to like her, so she couldn't relax."

"It can be hard to be the new kid," her mom agreed. "I'm glad you're so open-minded when you meet people and remember things like that," she added as she handed another salad plate to JoJo. "And it's nice to have different kinds of friends."

"Oh, for sure," JoJo agreed. "Not everyone is as outgoing as I am or as Miley is. Jacob isn't exactly outgoing, but he's super confident and chill. It's cool to have friends with different personalities. We go together like all the different ingredients in a salad," she added thoughtfully. "Speaking of which . . . Mom, pay attention!" she said in a pretend stern voice. "This one has a chunk of tomato on it!"

"Just seeing if you're on top of your job," her mom joked as she took the plate back.

JoJo rolled her eyes and stuck out her tongue, and her mom swatted her arm playfully. She loved this time with her mom—they had some of their best talks while doing the dishes together!

CHAPTER 5

JoJo was busy over the next few days practicing for her performance at the block party. She and Miley got together to work on possible routines. JoJo still wasn't sure which song she wanted to perform—"Kid in a Candy Store" or "Boomerang"—so they worked on new routines for both songs. It was a lot of work, but JoJo loved every minute of it. She'd been dancing since she was really little, and she'd known even back then that she wanted to be a pop star. She was living her dream now, and that took a lot of hard work and practice, but for JoJo, it was all worth it.

In between working, JoJo and Miley discussed the meeting at Kyra's house. Like JoJo, Miley had sensed that Kyra had been a bit on edge. The two friends agreed that what Kyra probably needed was to spend more time with them so she could relax and get to know everyone. That's when JoJo had another amazing idea—she would invite everyone over later that week to watch the two routines she and Miley had worked up. They could all hang out and help her decide which song to perform!

"I can't believe the block party is in one week," JoJo was saying between gulps of water. She put her glittery turquoise water bottle down and fanned her face with her hands. It was Saturday afternoon, and she had just finished performing her two new routines for Miley, Jacob, Grace, and Kyra.

"I can't believe how amazing your two routines are," Kyra said, her eyes wide. "I mean, JoJo . . . just, wow! I don't know how you'll ever choose which one to perform!"

"Seriously." Grace nodded. "They are *so* good! I love both songs, and the new routines are just so fantastic!"

JoJo beamed and held up her hand to high-five Miley. "Props to my BFF for the amazing routines!" she exclaimed. "I told you guys she was the best."

"Aw, thanks, girl." Miley grinned back. "It definitely helps to be choreographing for someone who's crazy enough to learn *two* new routines in one week!"

JoJo led everyone down to the basement, which was one of her favorite places to hang out when she had friends over. With arcade games, a giant-screen TV, and a Ping-Pong table, there was plenty of stuff to do.

"Believe it or not, this used to be my dance studio when I was little," JoJo told Grace and Kyra, pointing to a section of the finished basement that had a wall of mirrors. "Before my brother and dad converted it into their man cave, I used to come down here every single day to practice!"

"That's why she's so good," Miley added. She and Jacob had known JoJo for years, even back before the basement had a man cave. "Practice makes perfect!"

Just then, Jayden came downstairs. He said hello to Miley and Jacob and greeted Grace and Kyra warmly after JoJo introduced them.

"Mom wants to know if everyone wants to stay for dinner—she said we could order pizza."

"Oooh, I'm in!" Miley exclaimed.

"I'd love to—I'll text my mom and ask if I can stay," Kyra replied, her eyes shining with excitement, fingers flying over her phone screen.

"Me too," Grace added, pulling her phone out of her bag. JoJo couldn't help but notice her adorable unicorn phone case.

"I already know I have to be home for dinner," Jacob grumbled. "My mom told me before I left."

"Maybe you're having pizza at home?" Miley asked hopefully.

"I doubt it. My grandparents are coming over, which means we'll probably be having meat loaf." Jacob sighed dramatically.

"Tough break, man," Jayden said sympathetically as he made his way back upstairs. "JoJo, just let Mom know the final head count when it's all figured out," he called over his shoulder.

"What if this was my last chance to eat pizza before B-Day?" Jacob asked sadly. "B-Day" was how Jacob had begun referring to the day he was getting his braces put on, just less than a week away.

"You can eat pizza with braces," Grace assured him.

"Whew! I hope it tastes the same. Who wants to play Ping-Pong?" Jacob asked, grabbing a paddle. "Maybe pounding away at the little plastic ball will make me feel better!"

"I'll play!" Kyra and Grace exclaimed at the exact same time.

"You go ahead," Grace said quickly. "I'll play whoever wins."

As Kyra and Jacob played, Grace and Miley cheered from the couch while JoJo ran upstairs to talk to her mom. Kyra was really good; she was scoring point after point as the girls clapped.

JoJo came bounding back down the stairs a few minutes later, a huge grin on her face. "Time-out?" she said, and signaled to Kyra and Jacob. They both put their paddles down.

"I just asked my mom if you guys could sleep over tonight too, and she said okay!" JoJo bounced up and down on her toes in excitement. "So this can be a pizza party slash sleepover slash best night ever!" she exclaimed. "Oh, sorry, Jacob," she added. "Sad face for you!"

"Ugh, this is not my day," Jacob said, groaning. He picked up his paddle and made a funny face at Kyra. "Ready to finish killing me?"

"I am! Don't think I'm going to go easy on you because of the meat loaf," Kyra teased. And sure enough, she went on to beat him.

Jacob put his paddle down on the table. "I know when to accept defeat," he said solemnly. "All hail Kyra, the queen of Ping-Pong."

"Just call me Queen for short." Kyra giggled.

"We'll see about that!" Grace said, laughing. She jumped up and grabbed Jacob's paddle. "We have a table at my house too, so I'm not terrible. I challenge you for your crown!" she joked, smiling at Kyra.

"Oooh . . . this is getting serious!" JoJo crowed. "It's on!"

Miley, Jacob, and Grace were all smiling and laughing, but Kyra's face clouded over. She put her paddle down.

"I don't really feel like playing anymore," she announced flatly.

"Oh, I was only joking!" Grace said, a stricken look on her face. "I'm actually terrible at Ping-Pong. My five-year-old brother is better than me—"

"No, it's not that," Kyra interrupted. "I just don't feel like playing anymore. Besides, I think I heard my phone ding. It must be my mom texting me back."

Everyone waited while Kyra checked her phone. There was tension in the air all of a sudden, when just moments before everyone had been laughing and having a great time.

"I don't believe this," Kyra mumbled as she stared at her phone. "Be right back. I have to go call my mom," she said, and she ran upstairs.

Just then, Grace's phone dinged. "My mom said I can stay for pizza," she told JoJo softly. "Should I ask about sleeping over or not . . . ?"

JoJo could tell Grace's feelings were hurt by the way Kyra had just rejected her, and she felt terrible about it. She also had no idea what had just happened. But she wanted to fix it. "Of course you should ask her!" she said.

"Absolutely," Miley added, nodding.

"She said okay," Grace said a moment later. "Thanks so much . . . I—I hope Kyra won't mind . . ."

"You hope Kyra won't mind what?" Kyra asked as she appeared at the bottom of the steps, her hands on her hips.

"Oh, nothing," Grace replied. Her cheeks turned red, and she lowered her head, allowing her hair to cover her face.

"My mom said I can't stay," Kyra told JoJo. "She said I have to go home and work on stuff for the block party." She sighed angrily. "She said I *have other commitments*," she added, using air quotes.

"Is there anything we can help you with?" Grace asked.

"I told you, I can do it all myself!" Kyra snapped. Then she softened her tone as she turned to JoJo. "I'm just so sorry I can't stay."

"Hey, no big deal," JoJo said, thinking to

herself that it was probably for the best that Kyra couldn't stay that night. "Maybe we can do it another time," she added, catching the disappointed look on Kyra's face.

"Really?" Kyra said, looking hopeful. "That would be great! Maybe after the block party instead of tonight? Does that work for everyone?" She looked around the room.

"Oh, well . . ." JoJo cleared her throat. "Miley and Grace are still staying over, since they're free tonight," she explained. "I meant, maybe you can join us the next time."

"Oh, I see," Kyra said, her voice flat again. "Well, I guess I should just go, then. I'll text you guys about our next meeting for the block party planning. Have a fun sleepover."

With that, she grabbed her bag and flew up the stairs, leaving JoJo, Grace, Miley, and Jacob watching her in bewilderment. What had just happened?

CHAPTER 6

"You're not going to believe this, but I think I'm hungry again!" Grace exclaimed.

"Oh, I believe it," JoJo replied. "All that dancing works up an appetite—you should see me put away ice cream after a long day of dancing!"

"Speaking of which . . . ," Miley said, waggling her eyebrows. "Is the Siwa freezer as well stocked as usual?"

"You know it!" JoJo exclaimed.

The girls hurried to the kitchen, where Jessalynn Siwa was putting together the coffeepot for the morning. "Let me guess." JoJo's mom grinned as she looked at JoJo and her friends. "Based on the music we heard blasting upstairs and the fact that you all have red faces at ten at night, I'm betting you girls just finished a dance party and worked up an appetite. Am I right?"

"Yep," JoJo replied as she pulled pints of ice cream out of the freezer and placed them on the counter. "Ice cream sundae time!"

Mrs. Siwa pulled bowls down from the cabinet and placed sundae toppings on the counter next to the ice cream containers. "So, what else have you girls been up to tonight?" she asked as she collected spoons and an ice cream scooper from a drawer near the sink.

"Grace drew my portrait," JoJo said

excitedly. "Actually, she drew me *and* Bow-Bow. Hang on, I'll go get it so you can see it." With that, JoJo dashed out of the room and ran up to her bedroom.

"Here you go—careful not to get ice cream on it!" JoJo said a few moments later as she handed the portrait to her mom.

"Wow, Grace, you are really talented!" Jessalynn exclaimed as she turned on another light in the kitchen to get an even better look at the drawing. "This is wonderful—you captured JoJo's smile perfectly—and look at how cute BowBow looks! How long have you been drawing?"

Grace blushed happily at the compliments and carefully placed her spoon on the edge of her bowl. "I've always loved art, and my big sister, Megan, is a *really* good artist. She taught me to draw portraits. She's going to go to art school in Rhode Island this fall."

"I didn't know you had a sister," JoJo said between bites of cookies and cream. "I know you mentioned you had a little brother, but I didn't realize you had a sister too."

"Yeah, she's the best." Grace's face lit up. "She's already in Rhode Island—she spent the summer there, working and getting ready to start college," she explained. She picked up her spoon and began swirling it around in her ice cream. "I miss her a lot."

"I bet she misses you too," Jessalynn said, smiling kindly at Grace.

A few minutes later the girls finished up their sundaes, and Jessalynn announced she was going to head up to bed. "Have a great rest of the night," she said, kissing JoJo and BowBow goodnight. "And try to get *some* sleep—maybe no more dance parties tonight, okay?"

A short while later, the girls and BowBow were all settled on the floor of JoJo's bedroom. JoJo had a trundle bed, which was a bed with another mattress hidden underneath that could be pulled out when she had a guest. She usually used that when Miley slept over. But since she had two guests tonight, they had decided that all three of them would sleep on the floor. JoJo had piled pillows from her bed—luckily, she had a ton of them, because she loved throw pillows—all over the floor, and their sleeping bags were rolled out on top of a pile of thick comforters that were stacked one on top of the other.

"I feel like the princess and the pea," JoJo joked as she wiggled around on top of her sleeping bag. "So many layers!"

The girls weren't quite ready to go to sleep yet, so they were on top of their sleeping

bags instead of in them. JoJo had music playing but kept the volume low so they wouldn't
disturb her parents. She figured Jayden was
probably still awake, so she wasn't worried
about bothering him.

"Okay, I have to ask you," Miley said to
Grace. "Are unicorns your favorite thing?"
She gestured to the unicorn pajamas Grace
had changed into for bed. "I know you had a
unicorn shirt on the day I met you, and then
that necklace I totally want to borrow . . . and,
come to think of it, you've had something
unicorn on every time I've seen you!"

"Yeah, I love unicorns," Grace replied,
blushing slightly. Even though she was so
much less shy than she had been when
they first met, JoJo had noticed that Grace
still got a little uncomfortable sometimes
when attention was focused on her. "Do you

guys . . . um . . ." She looked down and began absently tracing circles on her sleeping bag. "Do you guys think unicorns are dumb or babyish?" she asked finally.

"What?!" JoJo and Miley said at the same time.

"Okay, you first," JoJo said, nodding at Miley.

"Not. At. All!" Miley said. "Unicorns are *awesome*! And it's great that they are your passion! Everyone needs something like that! Mine is glitter, by the way." She held out her hands and wiggled her fingers, showing off her glittery blue manicure.

"What she said!" JoJo said firmly. "I happen to agree that unicorns are amazing, and it's great that you love them and like to wear one every day—you do you, Grace!"

Grace smiled gratefully as JoJo paused to choose her next words carefully. "But, anyway, if you love them, it doesn't really matter what *we* think. Did someone tell you unicorns were dumb or babyish?" she asked softly.

Grace put her head down, and JoJo could see that her cheeks had turned red. She took a deep breath and then began to speak. "Yeah, some girls at my last school used to make fun of me for liking them," she said slowly. "They made fun of me for a lot of things, but my unicorn stuff was always something they teased me about. Part of me wanted to stop wearing them, but then the other part of me was, like, *why should I?*"

Grace looked up and saw that JoJo and Miley were listening closely, sympathetic looks on their faces. She continued. "So, as you can tell, I kind of had a hard time making friends at my old school. I used to get picked on a lot, and it was hard . . ."

JoJo reached out and squeezed Grace's hand. She wanted her to know she had friends and support.

"My sister used to tell me not to listen to the mean kids, that they were just bullies and I was special, like a unicorn," Grace added. "She used to tell me to imagine I had unicorn power to rise up above it all when kids were picking on me. Thinking about that always helps, and I guess that's why I always wear something with a unicorn on it . . . to remind me that my sister thinks I'm special."

"Coolest sister ever!" JoJo cried. "Oops, sorry, indoor voices! But seriously, I *love* that! And your sister is right—you are special!"

"Totally!" Miley cheered.

Just then, BowBow jumped up from her spot next to JoJo and ran over to Grace and hopped into her lap.

"See? BowBow knows!" JoJo smiled as the little Yorkie made herself comfortable.

Grace laughed and pet BowBow, who licked her hand. JoJo could tell she was feeling much better. She knew how special it was that Grace had chosen to confide in her and Miley.

"You know, what your sister told you sounds a lot like what the Siwanatorz stand for," JoJo said.

"Do you know about the Siwanatorz?" Miley asked Grace.

Grace shook her head, and JoJo continued. "Siwanatorz are like my fan army," she explained. "Siwanatorz stand for kindness. We stand up for each other and believe that bullying or being mean is *never* okay—like, not *ever*. We always have each other's backs."

"So we always have *your* back," Miley added.

71

"Oh, wow, that sounds amazing," Grace said. "I'd love to be a Siwanator too—what do I have to do to become one?"

"There's no special process or anything!" JoJo laughed. "You don't have to do anything. Just hang out and be yourself. Besides . . ." She pointed to her little dog, who had fallen asleep in Grace's lap and was snoring softly. "I think BowBow has already decided you are one!"

CHAPTER 7

From the way BowBow was barking in a corner of the room while JoJo practiced, she had a feeling her little pup was trying to tell her something. JoJo jogged over to her speakers and lowered the volume.

"What's up, BowBow?" she asked breathlessly.

BowBow yipped again, and JoJo's eyes fell on her glitter phone case.

"Is my phone blowing up?" she asked.

JoJo's suspicions were confirmed when she saw that she had two missed calls from Miley, as well as a text that read, *Call me!*

"Miley, I just got your text," JoJo said a moment later at the exact time that Miley said, "JoJo, did you get my text?"

"Jinx!" JoJo laughed. "So what's up?"

Miley explained that she'd gotten a text from Kyra saying she wanted them to come over that afternoon to check in on how things were going for the block party, which was just three days away.

"Did she ask you to include Grace too?" JoJo asked.

"No." Miley's voice was uncharacteristically serious. "She just mentioned you and Jacob. But I already texted Grace anyway— I mean, she's as much a part of the block party as we are! I'm not going to Kyra's without her."

"I totally agree." JoJo nodded. "I hope things are less tense this time than they were at my house last week . . ."

"Me too," Miley said.

"But no matter what, we've got Grace's back!" JoJo finished.

"Siwanatorz forever!" Miley cheered.

JoJo could tell Grace was nervous as soon as she came out her front door. Her red hair was in a cute side braid, and she wore a super cute, long-sleeve tee with a unicorn on it, but her expression was anxious, and her eyes were worried.

"I love your fishtail braid," JoJo said, grinning at her friend.

"Thanks." Grace smiled shyly and twirled her fingers through the end of her braid.

"Are you okay?" JoJo asked.

"I—I'm just . . ." Grace's voice trailed off.

They were only half a block away from Kyra's house.

"Hey, you guys go ahead, and we'll meet you there!" JoJo called to Miley and Jacob. They waved to let her know that was fine with them, and JoJo turned to Grace. "Talk to me," she said.

"I'm feeling nervous about going to Kyra's," Grace blurted out. "I know she doesn't like me, and I don't know why. I'm just kind of . . . scared that things are going to be super awkward again."

"I can understand why you feel nervous," JoJo said honestly. She fiddled with the end of her own ponytail as she thought about what else to say to Grace. "Things were a little weird at my house the other day. But I don't think you should be *scared*," she added firmly. "If, for whatever reason, Kyra has decided she doesn't like you, then that's *her*

problem, not yours. I know it can be hard, especially because you were bullied at your old school, but you just have to try to build a wall and block it out. That's what I do!"

"That's what *you* do?" Grace repeated, her eyes wide. "Who would ever make fun of you? I mean, you're, like, the coolest girl ever!"

"Right back at you!" JoJo said. "But believe me, I have been made fun of. People have said some really mean things about me online. It used to really upset me, but now I just don't pay attention to it. I built a wall around me, and I just block it out."

"Just block it out," Grace repeated. She took a deep breath. "I think I can do that!"

"*Won't let the haterz get their way . . . ,*" JoJo sang.

"*I'ma come back like a boomerang!*" Grace joined in.

"Yeah, high five!" JoJo cried. "And no matter

what, we all have your back! Never forget that!"

Wait, I thought your mom said Miguel was doing cotton candy while I did the snow cones," Jacob was saying to Kyra. "Is that a different Miguel?"

It was a little while later, and the group had been meeting to go over all the final details for the block party. They hadn't even gotten to JoJo's performance yet, and one thing was clear—a lot of details still needed to be worked out.

"No, it's the same Miguel," Kyra said with a sigh, and she scratched something out on her list. "I think—I'll figure it out."

"So if Miguel is doing cotton candy, then he can't do balloon animals, right?" Miley asked gently. "Can we help you find someone to do them?"

"Yeah, maybe my brother has some friends who can help out with the balloon animals," JoJo volunteered. "Want me to ask him?"

"No, I've got it all figured out," Kyra replied. "Thanks, though. Anyway, let's talk about your performance, JoJo. I think everything is all set," she added confidently.

"What about the flyer?" JoJo asked. "Did you just get a photo online or something? May I see it?"

"Oh." Kyra's face turned red; she had clearly forgotten all about the flyer. "I was saving the best for last!" she said quickly. "I'm doing it later today! I just need you to send me the picture you want me to use!"

Miley and JoJo exchanged a nervous look. It was *really* important to have a flyer with all the details about JoJo's performance. Otherwise, how would people know about it?

"Maybe we could help you out with the flyer," Miley said. "Because, you know . . . you have so much still to do."

"No, I've got everything under control," Kyra said, a tight smile on her face. "Besides, you have so much to do too, planning for your dance class! I'll figure it out!"

"I'd be happy to help with the flyer," Grace volunteered. JoJo grinned at her gratefully, and Grace took a deep breath. "I could work on it tonight and then send it to you, and—"

"I said, I have it under control!" Kyra snapped. "I don't need your help!"

"I just thought—"

Kyra kept right on talking, ignoring Grace. "Well, I think we've covered everything, so I guess I'll see you guys on Saturday! Let's all plan on showing up a little early, just in case . . ."

"Wait, we didn't talk about Grace's portraits," Jacob said.

"Oh, I forgot all about that," Kyra said, waving a hand dismissively. "You know . . ." She tapped her pencil on her pad. "I don't think we need them. I doubt if there will even be time for them . . ."

"Of course there's time for them!" Miley and JoJo cried in unison.

"Seriously, Kyra, Grace is *super* talented," JoJo said passionately. "I guarantee, her portraits will be a huge hit—we *have* to have them!"

"Fine," Kyra said, sighing. "You can do your portraits for two hours, at the end. Things will be slowing down at that point, anyway, since people will be getting ready for JoJo's performance."

"Why can't Grace do portraits all day?" Jacob asked. "The other stands will be open the entire day leading up to the performance, so why can't Grace's be?"

"I just don't think there will be that many people who want to get a portrait done," Kyra said firmly, tapping her pencil decisively as she spoke.

JoJo opened her mouth to say something, to tell Kyra she was being really unfair, but Grace caught her eye and shook her head as if to say, *It's okay.* JoJo did not like the way Kyra was acting one bit, but she was really glad to see that Grace didn't seem to be letting it get to her.

Grace's mom picked her up at Kyra's shortly after that—they had some errands to run—so JoJo, Jacob, and Miley left together to walk home.

"JoJo, don't forget to e-mail me the photo you want for the flyer as soon as you get home!" Kyra called as they walked down her driveway.

"I won't forget!" JoJo called back.

"Well, that was *interesting*," Jacob said as they rounded the corner.

"I was so proud of Grace," Miley replied. "She just let Kyra's behavior roll right off her!"

"And just wait until Kyra sees how talented Grace is," Jacob added. "Her portraits are going to be the hit of the block party! After your performance, that is," he said, nodding to JoJo.

"I think I know a way to kind of tie the two together, actually," JoJo replied, her eyes twinkling.

"Ooh, do tell," Miley said eagerly.

"Well, I decided what photo I'm going to send Kyra for the flyer. Except it's not a photo at all—it's a Grace Taylor, one-of-a-kind portrait!"

"Amazing idea!" Miley cheered.

"I know, right?" JoJo beamed. "I want to surprise her, though, so let's keep it between us!"

"And on that note," Jacob said, his eyes twinkling, "I'll see you guys on Saturday. But . . . does anyone want to wish me luck with what I'm doing the day after tomorrow?"

"What is he talking about?" Miley winked at JoJo.

"I have no idea," JoJo said with an exaggerated shrug.

"Really?" Jacob frowned. "You're messing with me, right?"

"Of course we're messing with you!" JoJo and Miley exclaimed in unison.

"Friday is B-Day!" JoJo grinned. "And to celebrate and wish you luck . . ." She dug through her backpack until she retrieved a paper bag that she and Miley had decorated with hand-drawn smiley faces with braces.

"We got you a little something to enjoy between now and then."

"There's every kind of chewy candy in here!" Jacob yelled in delight as he tore through the bag. "Laffy Taffy, gum, Starbursts, gummy bears, sour gummy worms . . . You guys are the best."

"Remember," Miley said, "you have to eat all that candy *before* you get your braces."

"A last hurrah," JoJo added.

From the way Jacob was grinning from ear to ear, JoJo knew they'd found the perfect way to let him know how much they cared.

CHAPTER 8

Saturday morning, the day of the block party, JoJo woke up earlier than usual. She was super excited about the block party and just a teeny bit nervous about her performance. But the butterflies in her stomach didn't bother her. JoJo had performed enough times to know that they would go away the moment she walked onstage. She loved performing and always felt great

doing it. She knew the butterflies were flut-
tering around from excitement just as much
as nervousness!

The smell of pancakes wafting up from
the kitchen officially lured her out of bed.

JoJo slid her feet into her favorite
slippers—fuzzy purple slides with silky bows
on top—grabbed her phone off her nightstand, just in case Miley was up early too and
needed to discuss any last-minute details for
their dance class, and headed downstairs.

In the kitchen, she found her mom and
dad at the table enjoying a pancake breakfast. "Good morning! Did the smell of pancakes wake you up?" her mom asked as she
pushed out the chair next to her to invite JoJo
to the table.

"You know it." JoJo yawned. "Works every
time!"

BowBow sniffed her slippers and looked up as if to say, *Where's my good morning?*

JoJo scooped BowBow up and gave her a good-morning kiss on the head, and Bow-Bow licked her cheek.

Sliding into the chair next to her mom, JoJo helped herself to a couple of pancakes, piled some strawberries on top, and then doused everything in plenty of maple syrup.

"Dee-lish," she told her mom between mouthfuls.

"We were just discussing how good the flyer for your performance looks," her dad said as he took a sip of coffee. "Your mom said your friend Grace drew the picture of you and BowBow? She's quite talented!"

"She sure is," JoJo agreed. She poured herself some orange juice. "I'm hoping that people will see the flyer and want to get their own portraits done by her. She'll have a stand at the block party, but only for a couple of hours, so make sure you get there early to get yours done!"

"Why such a short time?" her mom asked. "Once everyone sees this flyer, people will be lined up around the block to get their portraits done!"

"I know, right?" JoJo sighed. "There was some drama with Kyra, the girl organizing the events for the block party. She wasn't being very fair to Grace and didn't even want to give her stand a chance."

"That's a shame," her mom said, and her dad nodded. "I hope it doesn't make Grace doubt her own talent."

"I'm trying to make sure that doesn't happen," JoJo replied, and her parents smiled warmly. They were proud that JoJo was always there for her friends.

L ater that morning, JoJo was almost finished getting ready for the block party. She had the outfit she'd be performing in packed and ready to go in her backpack, and she was loving the outfit she'd chosen to wear beforehand: pale pink leggings, lilac Converse, and a peach, pink, and lilac polka-dotted T-shirt. Not only was the outfit super cute, it was also really comfy, so she could wear it for Miley's dance class. A matching peach bow completed the look. JoJo looked in the mirror and smiled . . . and as her eyes landed on the bow at the top of her side pony, she had a fantastic idea! She carefully removed the peach bow from her hair and scanned the dozens and dozens of bows that were attached to long ribbons dangling from hooks on her closet door. *That's the one,* she thought as her eyes landed on a pastel rainbow bow. The bow had long, glittery strands dangling down from it. The colors matched her outfit perfectly, but even better, the bow reminded her of a unicorn's mane, and by wearing it, she could support Grace by giving her an extra dose of unicorn power!

"So has anyone seen Jacob yet?" Miley asked breathlessly.

"Nope, but he texted me to say he'd be here in a few minutes," JoJo replied. "I can't wait to see his braces. I kept asking him to text me a selfie last night, but he said he wanted to unveil his new look in person."

"He told me the same thing." Miley laughed.

It was almost 11:00 A.M., and the block party was about to begin. As promised, JoJo, Miley, and Grace had all come early to help Kyra with any last-minute setup, but she was nowhere to be seen, so they were all hanging out near her face-painting stand. Grace's portrait stand was right next to it. Grace was already set up, even though her stand wouldn't be opening for a few more hours.

"Are you nervous about your performance later?" Grace asked JoJo.

"A little nervous, but it's a good kind of nervous," JoJo replied. She bounced on her toes. People were starting to show up already, and there was a buzz of excitement in the air. "I think I'm more excited than nervous!" she decided.

"I'm *super* excited!" Miley exclaimed. "I can't wait for everything to begin!"

"And I'm hungry," Jacob said.

The three girls spun around at the sound of Jacob's voice. They hadn't heard him walk up, but there he was, grinning broadly and showing off his brand-new, bright blue braces.

"You are totally rocking those." JoJo jumped up and down in excitement. "They look AH-MAZING! Right, guys?"

Miley skipped over and gave Jacob a hug. "They look *so* good on you, Jacob! Blue was a great choice!"

"They really do look great on you!" Grace agreed. "So, how did it go?"

"It was a lot better than I expected," Jacob replied. He was speaking just a little slower than usual, since he was still getting used to the feeling of braces. "All the stuff you told me about what to expect helped a lot."

Grace blushed happily. "I'm glad."

"I'm heading over to the food area now. My snow cone stand doesn't open until eleven thirty, but they might need me to sample the goods." Jacob rubbed his palms together in excitement. "See you guys later."

The girls all chuckled, and Miley checked

the time on her phone. "I promised my parents I'd meet up with them at eleven," she said. "See you soon for our dance class, JoJo?"

"You know it!" JoJo gave her best friend a thumbs-up.

"Good luck with your portraits, Grace!" Miley called as she walked away.

"I wonder where Kyra is," Grace said, looking around. "Her face-painting stand is supposed to open at eleven, but it's not even set up yet."

"Hopefully she'll get here soon," JoJo agreed.

"I meant to tell you, I love your bow," Grace said, pointing to the bow in JoJo's hair.

JoJo beamed. "Well, good, 'cause I wore it just for you!" she exclaimed. "It reminds me of a unicorn's mane, and—"

Just then, Kyra showed up. She was carrying a big box of supplies, and her face was flushed. JoJo thought Kyra looked *really* stressed out.

"Hey, everything okay?" JoJo asked.

"Yep, just setting my stand up," Kyra replied. She dropped the box down on the chair and began pulling out her paints and setting them up on the small table.

"Do you need help?" Grace asked kindly. "It's almost eleven, and a few people were by earlier, saying they'd be back at eleven . . ."

"I know what time it is, and I'm fine!" Kyra snapped.

JoJo watched Grace's expression and was relieved to see that she didn't seem to be taking Kyra's unfriendly tone to heart.

"Well, I'm here all day if you decide you need help!" Grace said simply. Then she turned to JoJo. "So, you were telling me about your bow . . ."

"Yes! Unicorn power!" JoJo laughed,

twirling one of the glittery strands from her bow around her finger. "And speaking of which, I'm loving your unicorn headband!"

"Thanks! My sister sent it to me," Grace explained, a smile lighting up her face. "I've never felt more like a unicorn," she said, reaching up the touch the pale purple satin horn attached to the headband. "I decided today was the perfect day to wear it, because I can use all the unicorn power I can get!" she finished, her gaze darting over to Kyra's stand. "I was up all night worrying that no one would show up for a portrait," she whispered to JoJo. "I'm excited, but, unlike you, I'm *super* nervous!"

"Well, then, I've got a surprise for you!" JoJo crowed. Now was the perfect time to show Grace one of the flyers. "Check it out," she said, pulling a flyer from her backpack.

"Wait—what? You used my drawing?"

Grace stared at the flyer JoJo was holding. "I can't believe you used the picture I drew for your flyer! You really think it's that good?"

"I *know* it's that good!" JoJo grinned. "People are going to be lining up to get their portraits done when they find out you drew this picture! The flyers are posted all over the place, on every block—everyone will see them!"

"I can't believe you used *my* drawing," Grace repeated. Her eyes were shining with happiness and pride. "It looks so amazing!"

"Excuse me, but why are you taking credit for the flyer that I designed?" Kyra demanded suddenly. She had been listening to JoJo and Grace's conversation.

"Because Grace drew the picture on the flyer," JoJo replied.

"I thought that was a professional drawing . . . ," Kyra mumbled, her eyes narrowing.

"Exactly!" JoJo said cheerfully. "I told you

she was super talented!" Then she turned her attention back to Grace. "I'm going to go meet up with my family for a bit so we can walk around together before Miley's dance class. Do you want to come?"

"My parents are meeting me here at eleven with my little brother. I promised I'd go with him to the bouncy house."

"Ah, good luck with that. Think of Jacob, and make sure he hasn't eaten a whole pizza beforehand!" JoJo joked. Then she turned serious for a moment. "But two things before I go: One, you got this! And two—unicorn power!"

"Yeah, unicorn power!" Grace cheered as JoJo walked away.

CHAPTER 9

"Here you go. I think you guys earned these," Jacob said, holding out two jumbo rainbow snow cones for JoJo and Miley. He was on his break from the snow cone stand and had watched the last few minutes of Miley and JoJo's dance class. It had been the biggest hit of the block party so far—even bigger than the bouncy house! More than twenty people showed up to take the class, and twice as many as that had gathered to watch once they realized that JoJo was helping teach the class. The neighborhood was full of JoJo Siwa fans of all ages! After the class, people had asked JoJo to pose for pictures. BowBow, who never missed an opportunity to look adorable, posed for some too.

"Miley, you did an amazing job of coming up with simplified versions of the routine for the beginners," JoJo said as she tightened the laces on her Converse. She stood up and bounced on her toes, still buzzing with energy from the class. "And some of the more experienced dancers were *really* good—my performance is going to turn into the ultimate dance party!"

"Yeah!" Miley crowed, high-fiving her best friend. "*We* were amazing!"

JoJo was more excited than ever about her performance. Meeting kids and adults from her neighborhood who were fans of hers had felt wonderful, and knowing that so many people couldn't wait for her performance had her feeling as if she might burst with excitement. Several kids had told her they considered themselves to be Siwanatorz, and that had made her day. JoJo loved meeting her fans! There was just one little detail she still needed to figure out: She needed to decide which song she was going to perform! Her fans had been pretty split down the middle, requesting "Kid in a Candy Store" and "Boomerang." Miley had taught dance routines for both songs during the dance class earlier, so JoJo knew her fans were prepared for whichever song she chose. It was a hard decision!

Just then, JoJo felt a gentle nudging at her ankles. She looked down and saw Bow-Bow holding something purple in her mouth. "BowBow, why do you have Grace's headband in your mouth?" JoJo wondered aloud as she bent over to retrieve it. "Oh, no!" she cried a moment later. The pretty satin horn on Grace's headband was covered in sticky black paint.

"Is that Grace's headband?" Miley asked, recognizing it from earlier.

"Yeah, I think it is. And it's ruined." JoJo frowned. "I'm going to go check on Grace and find out what happened. I'll catch up with you guys in a little bit, okay?"

"Yeah, sure. Text me if you need anything," Miley said, a concerned look clouding her features. Jacob nodded.

JoJo hurried over to the area where Grace's and Kyra's stands were. As she approached, she could see that Kyra wasn't around, but Grace was sitting on the chair at her stand, her head in her hands. It looked as if she was crying.

"Grace, are you okay?" JoJo ran the rest of the way to her friend. "BowBow brought me your headband. I'm so sorry it got ruined, but I bet we can fix it. My mom knows a bunch of cool tricks for getting stains out of my costumes, and—"

"It's not that," Grace said miserably. "Kyra did it—on purpose!"

"What?" JoJo exclaimed.

Grace nodded. "A little while after you left, things got really hectic with the face painting. There were so many people in line, and I think Kyra got really overwhelmed . . ." Grace's voice trailed off. "So anyway, people got tired of waiting in line and were leaving. A lot of them were coming over to *my* stand, asking when I was going to start doing portraits and asking if I could start early. It was making Kyra angry." Grace stood up and took a deep breath before continuing.

"Then, out of the blue, she asked me to come help her. I was really excited—I thought

103

maybe she'd decided to give me a chance. She asked to try on my headband, and when I gave it to her, she dropped it in a puddle of paint."

"Oh, Grace, I'm sorry . . . ," JoJo began.

"That's not even the worst part," Grace continued. "After she did it, she said now I wouldn't have unicorn power because my special headband was ruined and maybe I shouldn't do my portraits after all because I'd probably just mess them up."

"Listen to me," JoJo said, placing her hands on Grace's shoulders. "You are so talented, and your portrait of me and BowBow is the talk of the block party—people can't wait for you to open! Don't let Kyra get into your head."

Grace sighed. "Thanks, JoJo. It's just . . . now I'm even more nervous about doing the portraits. What if I mess up?" She gestured to the plain blue T-shirt she had on. "I don't have a unicorn anywhere on me—not even on my shirt. It feels weird. I don't know if I can do this without my unicorn power."

JoJo snapped her fingers. "I have an idea!" she cried. She reached up and gently removed the pastel rainbow bow from her side ponytail. Then she held the bow out to Grace and said, "Unicorn power."

"I—I can't take your bow!" Grace stammered.

"Of course you can!" JoJo said. "I'm *giving* it to you!"

"But you need a bow," Grace exclaimed. "You always wear one when you perform!"

"Yep, and I always pack a backup," JoJo explained.

"Thank you, JoJo," Grace said. She was beaming, and JoJo could tell she was feeling better. She just hoped that Grace could tune Kyra out and believe in herself as much as JoJo believed in her.

CHAPTER 10

It was a quarter to three, and Grace's portrait stand was due to open in fifteen minutes. There were already four people waiting to get their portraits done.

"Wow, look at the line you have already," JoJo said as she approached Grace's stand.

"Oh, hey!" Grace waved. "Did you try out the bouncy house?"

"I sure did!" JoJo sat down in one of the chairs at Grace's stand. "I got my bounce on, sampled the cotton candy, conquered the rock wall, played street mini golf, *and* I told everyone I met to make sure to get their portrait done at your stand."

"So in other words, you've been a little busy." Grace laughed.

"Yep." JoJo smiled. "I squeezed everything in so now I can relax a bit before I have to get ready for my performance. I'm supposed to meet back up with my mom in a few, but I just wanted to come say hello. Are you all set to open?"

Just then, the girls heard a commotion over at Kyra's stand. She'd returned with more supplies and knocked over the paints she'd set up on the wobbly table. She was covered in paint, and her stand was a mess.

JoJo and Grace rushed over to help. "Can we help you clean up?" Grace asked.

Kyra looked up, and JoJo held her breath. Was Kyra going to snap at Grace again? Tell her to get lost? Spill more paint on her?

Then Kyra did the unimaginable: She burst into tears!

"Oh, don't cry!" Grace and JoJo exclaimed at the same time.

"We'll get this cleaned up really fast," JoJo said, pulling a tissue from a packet in her backpack and handing it to Kyra.

"Where can I find lots of paper towels?" Grace asked JoJo.

"Try the concession area," JoJo said after a moment. "Jacob is still working there, and he can give you a bunch."

"Be right back," Grace said, and she ran off.

JoJo pulled the rest of the tissues out of the tiny pack and began wiping up as much paint as she could.

Kyra cleared her throat. "Why are you being so nice to me?" she asked quietly. "I've been terrible to Grace, and I know she's your friend. Why are you guys even helping me?"

JoJo stopped cleaning for a moment and looked at Kyra. "Grace *is* my friend, and you have been pretty unfair to her, but being mean to you wouldn't be right either. Besides, that's not me." JoJo stood up and threw the wadded tissues into a nearby garbage can. "Can I ask you something, though?"

Kyra nodded.

JoJo took a deep breath. "Why *do* you treat Grace differently? It seems like you never gave her a chance."

JoJo bit her lip, waiting to hear what Kyra would say. She knew that, a lot of times, bullies didn't even know why they were picking on someone. She had a feeling that whatever was bothering Kyra, it had way more to do with Kyra than with Grace. But would Kyra ever admit that?

"You're right. I never really gave her a chance," Kyra replied, sighing heavily. She began picking up jars of paint as she spoke. "I was so excited that day you guys all came over to talk about the block party. I wanted you guys to like me, and I was hoping you had room for another friend . . ." Kyra's voice trailed off. "And then you showed up with Grace, and I felt like she'd taken the spot I was hoping to get. I was mad, and I guess I was jealous," she finished softly. "Does that even make sense?"

JoJo sat on one of the chairs and patted the one next to her for Kyra to join her. "I guess so," she said slowly. JoJo understood what Kyra was saying, but she also knew it didn't have to be that way. She thought for a moment about how to explain that to Kyra. "You know, it's not like there's a limit to the number of friends we can have. And Grace is a really great friend." She met Kyra's eyes. "You're missing out."

Kyra swallowed and nodded. "I know. And I've been so horrible to her. Do you think it's too late? Do you think she'd accept my apology?"

"I honestly don't know," JoJo said gently. "But my mom always told me that you don't apologize to be forgiven. You apologize because it's the right thing to do."

Kyra nodded. "My mom says that too." She laughed. JoJo was glad to see that Kyra seemed to be feeling a bit better. "Do you think you could leave me alone with Grace when she gets back?" Kyra asked. "So I can try to talk to her?"

"I have to go warm up soon anyway," JoJo said, standing up. "My mom is probably wondering where I am."

Just then, Grace arrived back at the stand, breathless and holding a huge stack of paper towels. "Oh, you look better!" she said to Kyra when she noticed that Kyra was no longer crying.

"Yeah, I'm feeling a lot better. May I talk to you for a minute?"

Grace looked curiously at JoJo.

"I have to go find my mom," JoJo said. "But come by when you're done to say hi before my performance, okay?"

"Definitely," Grace agreed.

JoJo gave her friend a hug. "You've got this, Grace," she whispered in her ear. "Unicorn power! Text me if you need me, okay?"

As JoJo walked away, Grace placed a wad of paper towels on the table at Kyra's stand and began wiping up some spilled paint. She knew JoJo wouldn't leave her alone with Kyra if she thought there was a chance Kyra would be mean again. Thinking about that gave Grace a surge of confidence. "So what did you want to talk to me about?" she asked Kyra, careful to keep her voice even.

"I'm so sorry about before. About everything," Kyra blurted. "For ruining your headband, for not letting you help with the block party . . ." Kyra took a deep, shaky breath, unsure if she could continue, but then she thought about her conversation with JoJo and plunged ahead. "And most of all, for not giving you a chance. I am so sorry."

Grace stopped cleaning and straightened up. "Thank you for the apology," she said after a moment. "I appreciate it." Still a little uncomfortable, she looked at the ground.

"When does the face painting reopen?" a woman's voice rang out. Grace and Kyra looked up and saw a young woman with a toddler in a stroller. "Lila wants a mermaid! Do you do mermaids?"

"Um, I can try!" Kyra replied. "Just give me one minute, okay?"

"I should head over to my stand anyway," Grace said. "Are you okay now?"

Kyra looked Grace in the eye. "Actually, I'm a mess," she started. "I screwed everything up with this block party. I never confirmed the kids for the balloon animals, so there wasn't anyone to do them. I tried to fill in, but I was terrible at them." She held out her hand and used her fingers to tick off all the things she had done wrong. "I also never reminded people to come early to set up, so a bunch of stands opened late. And my face painting is awful. Beyond awful. One little girl cried when she saw the mermaid I'd painted on her arm because she thought it was a shark! So I'd better up my game before I traumatize poor Lila over there."

Grace burst out laughing. "I'm sorry—

I don't mean to laugh, but that's pretty hilarious."

Kyra smiled a little bit. Then her smile got bigger, and before long she was laughing with Grace. "It *is* pretty hilarious," she agreed finally.

"Want to know what I think?" Grace asked. When Kyra nodded, she continued. "I think you have two hours left before JoJo's performance and then the movie after dark. Why don't you walk around and ask for help? This is a block party—people are here to have fun, and I bet there are great painters in the crowd, or people who know how to do balloon animals. You don't have to do it all yourself. And then you should go have some fun, because . . . well, you live here too!"

Kyra was silent for a moment, and then she nodded. "That is really good advice. Thank you."

"No problem," Grace said. She walked over

to her stand and pulled out her pad and pencils, ready to begin drawing.

"Oh, and, Grace?" Kyra swallowed and looked at the ground. "Maybe after, I can come back and get a portrait drawn? You're really good—I'd love to get one . . . I think it would be the perfect souvenir from the block party."

"You got it!" Grace beamed.

"You're my last client of the day," Grace joked to Kyra. It was almost two hours later, and Grace's portrait stand had been a huge hit. She'd drawn so many portraits, she'd lost count! The art teacher from the high school even sat for one and told Grace she couldn't wait to have her in class in a few years because she was *that* talented. Grace felt like she might explode with pride when the teacher said that.

"Thanks for squeezing me in," Kyra replied

as she sat on the chair opposite Grace. "Can I talk while you do this, or do I need to sit still?"

"You can talk if you want to," Grace replied. "I pretty much know what you look like, since we've spent so much time together."

"Yeah, not that it's been nice times, though . . . ," Kyra said. She cleared her throat and sat up a little straighter. "I wanted to apologize again. I am so sorry that I was so mean to you. You never did anything to me, and you definitely did not deserve it."

"Thank you." Grace looked up for a moment to meet Kyra's eyes. "I really do appreciate the apology," she said as she began sketching again. "I'm glad to know I didn't do anything . . . but can you tell me why? I mean, why don't you like me?"

Kyra took a deep breath. She knew that if she told Grace that she'd been jealous of her,

117

she might risk Grace never wanting to be her friend. But then she remembered what JoJo had told her about apologizing because it was the right thing to do and not just to be forgiven. Kyra knew JoJo was right. Grace deserved the truth.

"I *do* like you!" Kyra said firmly. "Especially now that I've gotten to know you a little better today. You're so nice," she added sincerely. "I just ... I ... I was jealous," she said finally.

"Jealous? Of me?" Grace couldn't believe it. "Why?"

"When I moved here last year, I didn't really make any friends at school. When I found out about the block party, I knew it would be a great opportunity to get to know Miley and Jacob and JoJo." Kyra fidgeted on her chair as she spoke. "I knew who Miley was from school—she was in a different class than me, so I didn't know her that well—but she's so cool and nice ... *every-*

one likes her. And I knew she was best friends with JoJo, and I was so excited to meet her. I wanted to be their new friend." She put her head down and then, remembering that Grace was drawing her portrait, looked back up. "And then you showed up, and they had already decided to be friends with you, and I . . . I was jealous that you'd met them first. I was afraid they wouldn't have room in their lives for another new friend."

Grace stopped sketching for a moment. "Wow, I never thought about that . . . ," she said slowly. "I just thought you didn't like me."

"Why wouldn't I like you?" Kyra asked. "I mean, you're nice and fun and funny . . . and a really great artist! I thought you must have known I was jealous all along . . ."

"Nope, not at all." Grace shook her head. "You know, we have something in common. I had a hard time making friends at my old school, and I was super nervous about moving here. I was so excited when I met JoJo. Not because of how famous she is, just because she was so nice and wanted to be my friend. I kind of couldn't believe it!"

"It *is* pretty amazing how nice she is!" Kyra agreed. "But, seriously—*you* are really great. It's no wonder JoJo, Miley, and Jacob chose you to be their friend."

Grace smiled as she started sketching again. "Here's the thing, Kyra." She looked up briefly to meet Kyra's eyes again. "It's not like JoJo and her friends can only have one new friend. I think they want to be friends with you too."

"Oh, I don't know," Kyra replied, her cheeks coloring. "JoJo actually said the same thing, but, I mean, after the way I acted . . ." Her voice trailed off.

Grace could tell that Kyra was really and truly sorry for how she'd behaved. And she knew right then that she could forgive her.

"You can take my word for it," Grace said after a moment. "One thing I know about my new friends is that they *always* have room for another friend. You can count on that!"

Grace's pencil finally stopped moving on the paper. She held the portrait out in front of her to give it a good look and then, deciding it was done, turned it around to show Kyra.

Kyra's face lit up with the warmest smile Grace had ever seen.

"I absolutely love it," she exclaimed. "Will you sign the bottom?"

"Oh, sure." Grace blushed. No one had ever asked her to sign one of her portraits. She took the picture back and wrote:

To my new friend Kyra. xoxo, Grace.

CHAPTER 11

"I think I'm going to see if I can use this portrait as my class picture," Jacob was saying. He held out his portrait for Miley and JoJo to see. "I mean, look at how good I look! Grace somehow made my hair look even cooler than it does in real life. And she captured my braces perfectly!"

"Wow, that's so good!" Miley agreed.

"Maybe you should take the picture to the hairdresser," JoJo teased. Jacob pretended to look wounded. "I'm kidding," JoJo assured her friend. "You know I love you . . . and your funky hair."

Jacob grinned as he ran a hand through his shaggy mop. "By this time next month, my hair will be all grown out, and you guys will see my creative vision."

"If you say so, Jacob," Miley joked.

JoJo and her friends were hanging out in the backstage area. JoJo and BowBow were due to perform in a few minutes. JoJo had just decided moments before that she was going to perform "Kid in a Candy Store." It had been a hard call to make—she loved all her hit songs so much.

"JoJo, Grace and Kyra are here and wanted to say a quick hello before you go onstage," her mom said, walking toward them.

For the hundredth time that hour, JoJo wondered how things had gone between Kyra and Grace. She'd been dying to know if Grace was okay, but she also knew she had to give the two girls some space to talk things out on their own. She'd kept a close eye on her phone the whole time, just in case Grace had texted to say she needed her.

As JoJo caught sight of Grace and Kyra, she felt a rush of relief. They were both smiling as they approached the group.

"Hey, guys," JoJo said.

Before she could continue, Kyra spoke up.

"I wanted to apologize to all of you," she began. "I am so sorry that I've been difficult to deal with. I already explained this to Grace, but I was really jealous of her. I wanted to be friends with you guys so much that I got jealous of Grace for meeting you first and getting to be your friend." She stopped speaking and took a deep breath. "Now that I've gotten to know Grace a little bit today, I can totally see why you all want to be friends with her—she's amazing! She helped me out today even after I was horrible to her. She's a really good friend, and you guys are all lucky to have each other. So I just wanted to say I'm sorry and to let you know I won't act so mean anymore."

Miley, Jacob, and JoJo were silent as Kyra's words sank in. JoJo looked at Grace and could tell that she had forgiven Kyra. If Grace could forgive Kyra, then JoJo knew she could too.

"Um, I guess I'll be going now, but I can't wait for your performance, JoJo," Kyra added. She started to walk away, but JoJo called her back.

"So, I was telling Kyra earlier . . . ," JoJo said, looking at the faces of her friends, new and old, "that there's always room for new friends, right?"

"That's right," Grace cheered.

"Definitely," Miley agreed, her arms outstretched.

"Ugh, are we all going to hug now?" Jacob joked.

"JoJo, time to go!" Jessalynn called.

"One second!" JoJo called back. She scooped up BowBow so she could be part of the group hug with her friends. Just as they were pulling apart, Miley put her hand in the center of the circle, and the rest of the friends did the same. "What's going on?" JoJo asked. Then she realized. She placed her hand in the center of the circle and beamed with excitement as her friends all cheered, "Go, JoJo and BowBow!"

JoJo and BowBow waited just offstage. Kyra's mom, the head of the block party committee, was onstage introducing JoJo.

"Before we bring out the biggest star of our neighborhood, I wanted to thank my daughter, Kyra, for organizing the entertainment for this block party. Kyra, can you come up here for a moment?"

JoJo cheered as Kyra slowly made her way onstage. She looked really nervous. JoJo got it;

the first time you stared out at a sea of faces from a stage was a moment you never forgot!

Borrowing the microphone from her mom, Kyra cleared her throat and spoke slowly and carefully. "My mom put me in charge of the entertainment, but the truth is, I never could have done any of it without the help of my friends," Kyra said, her voice shaking ever so slightly. "So I'd like to thank JoJo, Miley, Jacob, and Grace. Especially Grace—she's the one who drew all those amazing portraits!" Kyra paused as the crowd cheered for Grace. The cheers kept going until Grace finally came up onstage too. She linked arms with Kyra, and the two friends took a bow together.

JoJo clapped from her spot offstage, and BowBow barked her approval.

"And now, without further ado . . . ," Kyra's mom said. "The moment you've all been waiting for . . ."

127

JoJo felt the electric buzz of excitement ripple through her. She couldn't wait to perform. And, as she ran onstage, she had an amazing idea. In that exact moment she knew for sure which song she wanted to perform, and it wasn't "Kid in a Candy Store" after all.

She grabbed the microphone and instead of immediately bursting into song, she cleared her throat and waved to the audience. The crowd went wild.

"Wow, thank you!" JoJo grinned. She could see her friends and family in the front row.

"It feels amazing to be out here, ready to perform at home. Thank you so much for coming!"

The crowed exploded with applause. It was so loud, it sounded like thunder! "And before I begin, I want to dedicate this song to my two newest friends—Grace and Kyra. Guys, this one's for you!"

And then JoJo broke into "Boomerang,"

because she had realized while she watched her friends from backstage, *both* girls had done a pretty amazing job of coming back . . . just like a boomerang!

As JoJo sang, it became clear that the crowd was not going to be finished dancing after just one song, so she kept going. She broke into "Kid in a Candy Store" and pulled Miley, Grace, Kyra, Jayden, and several of the kids from the dance class onstage. Even Jacob, who didn't really like to dance, hopped onstage and danced around. After "Kid in a Candy Store," JoJo kept going. She performed "Hold the Drama," "Every Girl's a Super Girl," and then ended with an encore of "Boomerang." The whole block was dancing and laughing and singing, and JoJo never wanted it to end. She'd always thought that nothing could top the rush she got from performing. But doing it at home, with her friends, family, and fans onstage with her—that was the best feeling in the world.

Read on for a sneak peek from

JoJo & BOWBOW
CANDY KISSES

CHAPTER 1

"I've got to try the special of the day—the heart-shaped pancakes," JoJo Siwa said, grinning at the waitress as she scribbled away on her notepad. "With strawberries and whipped cream and chocolate sauce." The waitress nodded, giving JoJo a smile. "Oh, and a glass of orange juice, please!"

"I'll have a cup of coffee and the stuffed French toast," Jessalyn Siwa said, closing her menu and placing it on the table.

"Mom, how can you pass up the chance to have heart-shaped pancakes? I mean, they only come around once a year!" JoJo exclaimed as the waitress walked away. "It's almost Valentine's Day! Heart-shaped foods should be eaten as often as possible!"

"Well, technically, Valentine's Day is still almost a month away," Jess replied, laughing. "Plus, I figured I'd just have a bite of yours."

"*If* I let you." JoJo wiggled her eyebrows. "I'll probably want it all to myself. . . ."

"No problem," Jess said. "That's sort of how I'm feeling about my French toast. Remember French toast? Your favorite breakfast when heart-shaped pancakes aren't on the menu? Don't worry, I'm sure I can handle it on my own."

"Correction: French toast is my favorite when heart-shaped pancakes *and donuts* aren't on the menu! But fine. You win. We'll share." It was a game they always played—but they both always wound up sharing. JoJo knew the real reason her mom had ordered the stuffed French toast was because she knew how much JoJo loved it and she planned on sharing it with her all along. It was just one of the many things JoJo loved about her mom.

S peaking of love . . . JoJo *loved* Valentine's Day. It was one of her favorite holidays, right up there with Christmas, Halloween, and her birthday. And BowBow's birthday, of course. BowBow was JoJo's adorable teacup Yorkie.

"We should talk about Valentine's Day, actually," Jessalyn said, taking a sip of her water. "Your dance workshop will be ending on Valentine's Day, right? It's going to be a very busy few weeks between now and then."

"That's right," JoJo replied. "You know, on second thought, I'm in no rush for it to get here. I don't want my class to go by too quickly. I can't believe it's finally about to start! It feels like I auditioned a million years ago. . . ." JoJo paused as the waitress came by the table to drop off their beverages. "I'm still so excited I made it into the class!"

"It's definitely an honor to have gotten one of the spots," Jessalyn agreed as she poured a little milk into her coffee. "But I'm not surprised. You've worked so hard for this."

JoJo had auditioned for the dance workshop back in November. There were only ten spots available in the four-week class, which was an immersive multidisciplinary workshop being taught by one of the most famous retired choreographers in the world. Dancers of all ages, from all over the country, had auditioned to be accepted into the workshop.

The spots were all awarded on a scholarship basis, which meant the workshop was free to anyone who made it in. JoJo had been ecstatic when she'd received word that she'd earned one of the coveted spots in the workshop and had been counting down the days until it all began. She'd even circled the day in fluorescent-pink marker on her calendar and drawn a bunch of hearts around it. And now the big day was finally here!

"I can't wait to see who else will be in the program," JoJo said, drumming her fingers on the table excitedly. "And what kind of dancers they will be. I remember there were a bunch of classically trained ballerinas at the audition when I was there. I hope some of them made it in—it would be so cool to be dancing alongside professional ballerinas!"

JoJo had plenty of experience with dance classes, since she'd been performing pretty much her whole life—first for fun, and now professionally. She'd gotten an extra-early start, dancing on stage for the first time when she was just two years old! JoJo always felt right at home in dance class. She couldn't wait to meet the other dancers in the workshop and experience what she was sure was going to be one of the most exciting and challenging opportunities of her life.

"I would imagine there will be dancers from all disciplines," Jessalyn said, sipping her coffee. "And I also wouldn't be surprised if you are one of the youngest dancers in the workshop, if not *the* youngest." Her mom put her mug down. "It's a good thing you're used to being the youngest dancer surrounded by older ones."

"True," JoJo nodded. "I'm always up for making new friends and adding some big sisters to my dance family." Her eyes twinkled, and she bounced in her seat. She was so excited it was hard to sit still!

Just then, the waitress appeared at the table and plunked down two heavy plates. Jessalyn's plate held two giant pieces of French toast sprinkled with powdered sugar and oozing maple syrup; but JoJo's plate was nothing short of spectacular. JoJo inhaled the wonderful, sweet scent of pancakes and admired the perfect heart-shaped stack loaded with strawberries and fudge sauce. Her stomach growled just looking at it.

"I have to take a picture of these to send to Miley," she said. The pancakes smelled even better than they looked, which was really saying something. A couple of the strawberries had been cut so they fanned out and formed little rose-shaped garnishes.

JoJo snapped a picture of her beautiful breakfast and quickly sent it off to her BFF with some heart emojis. Miley was in school, so JoJo knew she wouldn't be able to reply to the text for a while, but she also knew Miley would be happy to have a text waiting for her later. Unable to wait even one more second, JoJo took an enormous bite.

"Well, are they as good as they look?" her mom asked while JoJo chewed.

JoJo nodded and widened her eyes to show her appreciation. "They. Are. Amazing," she said once she finally swallowed. "Give me your plate."

"Only if you'll take a piece of this ridiculously amazing French toast," her mom said, cutting off a generous wedge. "Today we're celebrating."

"Deal," JoJo giggled, trading her mom a

wedge of her pancakes for the syrupy French toast. "I'm going to need all the energy I can get today!"

"BowBow, any last words of wisdom before I leave for class?" JoJo asked.

A few hours later, JoJo was relaxing with BowBow in her pink-and-teal bedroom. It was almost time to leave for dance class. The morning had seemed to crawl by after breakfast. JoJo had completed all of her homeschool assignments for the day, then changed into her favorite sparkly dancing gear for class. After debating back and forth about which bow gave her the perfect "first day of dance workshop" look, JoJo had finally settled on black with clear rhinestones. It was one of her favorites, and it looked really cute with her black leggings and hot-pink, sequined top.

"Um, excuse me. BowBow! I asked you a question. . . ."

As if on cue, BowBow yipped.

"That's excellent advice!" JoJo cried, scooping up her little dog up and giving her a kiss on the head. "I will definitely make sure to have *the best* time!"

JoJo placed BowBow back on the ground and took one last look around her room to make sure she had everything she needed. She triple-checked her backpack, making sure her lucky water bottle was there, along with her favorite hair ties. She was pretty sure she had everything. She caught a glimpse of herself in the mirror that rested over her dresser and gave it a smile. "Let's do this," she told her reflection. She looked sparkly. She looked good. She looked like a dancer who was ready for anything.

MORE BOOKS AVAILABLE BY JOJO SIWA!

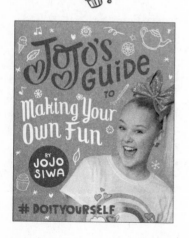